THE
PRINCESS,
THE
COWBOY
AND THE WITCH WHO STOLE
THE MAGIC SNOW GLOBE

ELIZABETH O'BRIEN

*Paige,
thank you for
buying my book!
I hope you enjoy
the adventure!*

ILLUSTRATED BY
RICHA KINRA

outskirtspress

DENVER, COLORADO

Chapter 1
The Ball

The kingdom of Wonder Valley shimmered beneath the moonlight. All sorts of wild flowers surrounded the castle, and the wind swayed them back and forth elegantly. Within the castle, a ball was being held, and twelve princes from faraway lands came to meet Princess Ezrah. She had just turned eighteen and it was time to choose a prince to marry to help her rule the kingdom someday. Every prince took a turn dancing with Princess Ezrah, hoping to charm and persuade her to choose him to marry.

"I know you will pick me... I mean, really, why wouldn't you? I am the best-looking prince here," Prince Connell said to Ezrah, dipping her down and showing off his dance moves. Ezrah looked up at his prideful smirk and rolled her eyes.

Another prince butted in and began dancing with Ezrah. "Princess Ezrah, my name is Prince Richard." He then lifted her hand and kissed it. Ezrah pulled her hand away in disgust, wiping the spot off where he had kissed it with the sleeve of her dress.

"Many people call me Prince Rich for short, and I definitely live up to that name," Prince Richard said, and he laughed at his own cleverness. "I could give you anything you ever wanted. I own more land and gold than you can imagine." He continued to brag about all his possessions and the money he made.

Ezrah became very bored listening to Prince Richard. In fact, every prince she danced with she thought was boring. Ezrah just wanted the night to end. When the clock finally struck midnight, the king made the announcement that would grant Ezrah her wish.

"Thank you all for coming," the king said. "My daughter Ezrah will declare which one of you she will marry in two days at the Grand Dinner."

All the princes finally left, but before doing so, they all made sure they got Ezrah's attention by giving one last wink, smile, wave, or pursing their lips together as if they were giving her a kiss. Ezrah just slightly waved back, feeling annoyed yet relieved they were all finally leaving.

Before Ezrah's parents left the ballroom as well, they both came over to her to give her a hug and say good night. "I hope you choose wisely, my daughter," Ezrah's mother whispered in her ear before

parting from her embrace. And then they both headed for bed, leaving Ezrah alone with her white owl, Beeley.

"So whoooo will you choose?" Beeley asked from above, swooping down beside Ezrah and perching on one of the tall windowsills.

Beeley had been Ezrah's guardian since she was born. His white body with brown speckles was quite small in proportion to his oversized head and bulging blue eyes. His sole purpose was to watch out for Ezrah and help protect her from any harm. Everyone who was of royalty had some sort of animal as their own personal guardian. For Beeley, his job was rather challenging, because Ezrah often did whatever she wanted, when she wanted, no matter what anyone else thought about it.

"I don't want to marry any of them!" Ezrah huffed. "I don't know why I can't just rule this kingdom myself!"

Suddenly Ezrah turned around, for the sound of the ballroom's entry doors opening startled her. A tall, skinny man came walking through, rolling along with him a mop and a bucket. Ezrah folded her arms across her chest. "Umm...excuse me?" she asked in a rather rude tone. She wasn't in the mood for any more company.

The man looked over at Ezrah, but ignored her comment as he

began mopping the floor. He knew who she was. He lived in a village outside of the kingdom, and he as well as many of the village folk perceived Ezrah as a spoiled and conceited princess.

Ezrah was caught off guard by the man's actions. No one had ever ignored her, and she was sure he had heard her.

"Excuse me! Do you know who I am?!" Ezrah demanded.

The man answered yes, but continued mopping, never taking his eyes off what he was doing. Beeley flew over to the staircase and perched on the railing, staring at the two with his humungous round eyes. He knew this was not going to end well.

Ezrah became irritated and quickly walked over to him, grabbing the mop right out of his hands. "If you know who I am, it would be wise of you to acknowledge me when I am speaking to you."

The man stood tall in front of her and crossed his arms, staring at her and giving her his full attention. If she wanted to play her snooty little games, he was ready to play along.

Ezrah stared right back at him, looking into his deep bluish gray eyes as she waited for him to say something. But with the awkward silence, the fact that the man was incredibly handsome and somewhat intimidating had caused Ezrah to feel inferior.

"Well, don't you have anything to say?!" Ezrah finally blurted out.

The man stood there and scratched his head for a moment. "Can I have my mop back?"

Ezrah was flabbergasted. She let out a frustrated "Uh!" and told the man she had better things to do than linger with a commoner. She swung the mop out toward him, but in doing so, she tripped over the mop head. Instinctively, the man threw his arms out and caught her before she fell to the floor. Though there was nothing about the man that was entirely gorgeous like the princes she met at the ball, there was something about him that entranced her. At a loss for words, Ezrah couldn't help but stare into this man's beautiful blue eyes. They were so bright and clear she could easily see her reflection within them. The man couldn't help but stare into Ezrah's illuminating dark blue eyes as well. Finally after a few moments, the man carefully stood her back up on her feet.

"I gotta name," said the man, picking up his mop off the floor. "It's Jacob. I've worked for the kingdom for years takin' care of the horses, doin' maintenance work round the castle, and helpin' the maids after functions like you had tonight. What was it, the *Grand Ball?*"

Jacob said "the Grand Ball" with a little bit of mockery, and it made Ezrah irritated once again. "Why yes, it was the Grand Ball, and I am sorry you weren't invited. Generally these kinds of functions aren't suitable for commoners."

"Us commoners wouldn't have wanted to come to some boring Grand Ball anyway."

"Boring?!" Ezrah yipped. "They are far from boring."

"They couldn't be closer to boring. Even the dancing is boring."

"What would you know about dancing?" asked Ezrah.

"A whole lot more than any prince you danced with tonight," Jacob said proudly, and then just so he could prove himself, he offered his hand to Ezrah.

"It wouldn't be appropriate for me to dance with a…" but before Ezrah could finish her sentence, Jacob had already grabbed her and swung her around in circles. He kicked up his heels, swept her across the floor in a quick two-step motion, and took her hands in his as they bounced around the ballroom carelessly. The movements were so carefree and so unstructured that Ezrah couldn't help but let out a laugh, which she then tried to cover up with a cough. Beeley's eyes got wide as he watched from the staircase. Ezrah laughing? That wasn't something that anyone in the castle had heard for a long time.

Jacob ended with a dip and again they gazed into each other's eyes. Their stare was finally broken when Ezrah's father yelled for her.

"I have to go," said Ezrah.

"Ezrah! Where are you?" Ezrah's father called out.

"Coming!" Ezrah yelled back. "I guess you may know a little something about dancing," she said to Jacob, straightening the length of her dress and then whipping around to walk toward the ballroom doors. Jacob stood still, unsure what to say or do. He noticed something different about her when they were dancing. Maybe deep down she did have a fun side and kind heart, and wasn't just the snooty princess everyone thought she was.

Beeley flew from the staircase railing to follow Ezrah out. Jacob yelled a "good night," but Ezrah was already gone. Beeley turned his head around to look back at Jacob, and to Jacob's surprise, Beeley gave a big wink.

Chapter 2
Ezrah Runs Away

It was another serene morning in the kingdom of Wonder Valley. Beeley flew outside the castle walls and upward to Ezrah's bedroom. He entered her room through a large window she always left open for him, and he found Ezrah sleeping peacefully in her bed.

Ezrah awoke to Beeley's routine wake-up call of loud whooing, flapping wings, and staring at her with his enormous yellow eyes just inches from her face. Startled as usual, Ezrah quickly jumped out of bed, practically tripping over her own feet.

"Do you have to wake me up by freaking me out every time?" Ezrah asked.

"It works though, doesn't it?" asked Beeley, ruffling his feathers as he went over and perched on her bedpost.

Ezrah gave him a glare and rummaged through her oversized closet to find something to wear.

"So what are we going to do today, Princess?" Beeley asked.

Ezrah growled in frustration while she sifted through her crowded closet of dresses ranging from every color and style. "We are going into the city to buy a new dress! I've already worn all of these at least once."

Beeley was used to Ezrah's pointless quarrels and he had learned to tolerate them. "But how? You know your father won't allow you to leave the castle walls," he said.

"He won't have to allow it, because we aren't going to tell him. I am eighteen now. If I am old enough to help rule the kingdom, I am old enough to go out and shop in it."

Ezrah picked out a more casual dress that she had never worn; one that was hand sewn by one of the castle maids for her birthday. She then put a dark brown wig on and put it up in a ponytail. She was thankful she still had the wig from her younger days of playing "dress-up."

"Ugh. This dress is a perfect disguise. A princess wouldn't be caught dead wearing such a ghastly thing!" Ezrah said, looking in the mirror and making an ugly facial expression.

Beeley didn't like the idea of sneaking out of the castle, but Ezrah always got her way, and he knew there was no trying to talk her out of it. They both left her room and quietly descended the long staircase. When they reached the bottom, they froze after hearing the castle maids talking.

"I wonder which prince Ezrah will choose?" one maid asked the other.

"I don't know, but I feel terrible for the poor fool," the other maid answered. Both maids chatted away while dusting the pictures along the hallway walls.

"There definitely won't be a happy ending to their love story," one maid said.

"Love? I doubt Ezrah knows anything about love. She only has enough love for one thing….money."

Ezrah overheard every word the maids said about her. She became quite upset. She felt betrayed, yet deep down Ezrah knew there was some truth to what they had said. She did in fact love money. After the maids disappeared down the long hallway, Ezrah ran to the stone fireplace and filled a small bag with the black ash. She would use the ash to disguise her white horse, Tulip. Ezrah and Beeley then quietly snuck out the doors that led to the backyard.

Creeping behind trees and bushes, Ezrah made it past the two bobcats, Tony and Tray, who were the king and queen's guardians. They also helped protect the castle, watching out for any intruders.

Beeley flew to the top of an apple tree that they were lying under and began shaking the branches. Apples started to plummet to the ground and onto Tony and Tray, who had been resting below.

While Beeley was keeping them preoccupied, Ezrah went into the horse stable and got Tulip. She dusted him with the black ash from her bag and made black blotches on his hair. Ezrah didn't ride him very often, so she barely stayed on him as he ran out of the stables and around to the back of the castle. Tony and Tray didn't suspect anything going on in the barn. They were too distracted by the falling apples. Beeley saw Ezrah had made it out of the castle entrance and quickly flew after her. Tony and Tray stayed put, rubbing their throbbing heads with their paws.

"Stupid squirrels," muttered Tray, lifting his paw up and shaking it up at the tree.

Tony and Tray left the tree and went back to work scouting the castle walls and gates, unaware it had been Beeley behind the mischief.

Ezrah rode Tulip into the kingdom, passing numerous people on

THE PRINCESS, THE COWBOY AND THE WITCH WHO STOLE THE MAGIC SNOW GLOBE

the streets who hadn't a clue she was the princess. Her brunette wig, long blue cape, and casual blue dress kept anyone from recognizing her, although many gave her a curious glance. Ezrah made it to the street where all the clothing shops were and tied up Tulip. Walking down the street with Beeley flying high above her to keep out of sight, Ezrah overheard her name when she caught up to three young ladies who were gossiping amongst themselves, each carrying a bag of items they had purchased at various shops.

"I wish I was as rich as Ezrah. She probably doesn't have to lift one finger in that castle to do any kind of work!" the short woman with curly blonde hair said. "Lazy, spoiled, and greedy is what that princess is!" the taller woman said, sticking up her nose in the air. "When has she ever come out of her castle? She has everyone else doing things for her. I bet she's spoon fed!"

The three young ladies laughed hysterically. The last woman, who was short and chubby with brown wavy hair pretended to be Ezrah. She walked ahead of the other two with her head tilted back and moving her hips ridiculously from side to side. "Buy me a new spoon!" she yelled at the other two. "I am sick of silver! I want a gold one!"

The three laughed again and turned in to a small grocery shop on the right. Ezrah continued down the street, walking slow with her head down, staring at the ground in front of her. Ezrah never really cared what people thought about her. She always counted on *things* to make her happy, but she couldn't ignore what she was overhearing. She was beginning to feel lonely, realizing she had no one besides Beeley who she regularly talked to.

Ezrah found a dress shop and Beeley perched on the roof outside. She picked through one rack of dresses, but she wasn't much in the mood to shop anymore. The store clerk, a sleek older woman wearing all sorts of jewelry and looking a bit suspicious, approached her slowly.

"Can I help you find something?"

"I am just browsing," Ezrah replied.

Suddenly they both turned as a man walked in through the front doors. Ezrah thought he looked familiar, and when he lifted his cowboy hat to readjust it, she practically fell into the rack of dresses she was looking through. It was Jacob!

What is he doing here? Ezrah wondered.

"Uh...can I help you?" the store clerk finally asked, walking over toward Jacob and forgetting about Ezrah for the moment.

Ezrah pretended to look through another rack of dresses, curious to find out what Jacob was doing in the store.

"Well, I got two sisters and there's sort of a dance festival going on tonight in our village. Thought I might come get 'em somethin' nice to wear."

"How nice of you!" the store clerk said, delighted. "Okay, well, what is your price range?"

"Ain't too worried about the price, ma'am. I've been saving for quite some time. Jacob said.

"Do you know their dress size?"

"No, but they are twins and about yay high," Jacob said, lifting his hand just below his chest to indicate how tall they were. "Skinny little things too."

Why isn't Jacob's mom coming to pick out and buy the dresses? Does he not have a mom? Does he not have a dad either? Ezrah thought.

The store clerk picked out two very girly dresses, one pink and one purple, both ruffled at the shoulders and below the knees. Just after Jacob had left the store, the next customer that walked in happened to be Ezrah's mother! Ezrah quickly took her long bangs and draped them down the sides of her face. The store clerk looked over at Ezrah, as if checking to make sure she still didn't need any help. Ezrah smiled and nodded, reassuring her she was still just browsing.

"I've been waiting all day. Tell me, how did the Grand Ball go?" asked the clerk as she approached Ezrah's mother.

Ezrah moved closer and shuffled through some more dresses, hoping to persuade her mother and the store clerk she wasn't at all eavesdropping. But of course she was listening as carefully as she could, for they were talking just above a whisper.

"It was a very glamorous night," Ezrah's mother said, fiddling with some flowers that were arranged on the front counter, "but I can't help but find it all a bit unnerving."

What did she mean by that? Ezrah thought.

"You don't think Ezrah can handle the responsibilities?" the store clerk asked.

Ezrah's mother scanned the store, contemplating whether or not she should continue the conversation. She then leaned over the counter to get a bit closer to the store clerk as she spoke. But Ezrah had excellent hearing. It wasn't the first time she had eavesdropped on a conversation. It was one of her favorite hobbies.

"I think if our daughter's heart was in the right place, she could handle ruling the kingdom by herself, but we can't help but fear how her greed and selfishness would harm the succession of Wonder Valley if she were to rule on her own," said Ezrah's mother.

"You don't think she would change like Sheena did, do you?" the store clerk asked, raising an eyebrow.

Surely they couldn't compare her to Sheena, the evil witch! Ezrah remembered her mother and father telling her the story about Sheena and how she had been the king's friend long ago.

Sheena had helped the king with many decisions and responsibilities before he had met Ezrah's mother. But after a while, Sheena had become greedy and selfish, living such a luxurious lifestyle. She began obsessing over power and control, and stopped caring about anything else in the world. Eventually Sheena began despising things that were of true beauty, and she became evil. She told the king she wanted Wonder Valley's beauty to be covered with snow and be filled with coldness, but the king banished her from Wonder Valley, realizing she had changed and had become wicked.

"I don't believe my daughter would ever turn into something *that* evil," Ezrah's mother said confidently, but then with a sigh, "However, I do fear the kingdom would suffer in some way."

Ezrah stopped shuffling through dresses. She couldn't believe what she was hearing her mother saying about her and she quickly snuck out of the store. Ezrah suddenly felt all alone and wanted to escape; escape the life of a princess, even if it was just for a day. Getting back on Tulip, she remembered Jacob mentioning a dance festival being held in his village. She had a sudden urge to find out more about Jacob and his village. She decided it was the perfect place to run away to.

Riding along the back trails of the kingdom with Beeley flying above her, Ezrah found the wooden sign at the edge of the forest. It showed a map of the kingdom and surrounding towns. Ezrah looked harder and located the small village far across the other side of the forest.

"There!" Ezrah said aloud, pointing to the place on the map. "Golden Brick; that must be the village Jacob is from. Let's go." Ezrah got back on her horse while Beeley bent over the top of the sign, studying the map upside down. His eyes bugged out and he looked at Ezrah.

"This is too far, Princess! Who knows what weird and crazy creatures are lurking in that forest... Oh and your father? Well, he'd probably have me for a Thanksgiving turkey if I let..." Beeley rambled, but Ezrah interrupted.

"I am going with or without you, Beeley," Ezrah said, waving her hand up as they entered the forest. Beeley had no choice but to follow behind. He flew just above Ezrah and Tulip, his eyes wide and searching in every direction for any danger. The path narrowed, and the trees were so thick that daylight couldn't break through the tree tops. It almost appeared as though the forest had swallowed them up.

Chapter 3
Sheena's Spell

Sheena, the evil witch, groveled about Wonder valley, cursing its beauty and Princess Ezrah. She had jealousy in her heart so great it made her curse everything lovely.

Sheena walked up to her home with her rabbit Jakko, clumsily hopping behind her. Sheena stopped abruptly as she caught sight of a newly bloomed flower. Her eyes grew wide and she clenched her fist, boiling with anger over the single flower that had somehow managed to sprout up. Only poisonous plants and weeds of all kinds surrounded her home, which was a large hollow tree.

Sheena ripped the flower from its stem and held it between the palms of her hands. She furiously rubbed her hands back and forth, shredding the flower to pieces, and stomping on the remains of petals that scattered the ground.

"If I could just find a way to sneak into the castle and get a hold of that snow globe, I'd create a storm and rid Wonder Valley's beauty once and for all!" screamed Sheena. Though she was actually quite beautiful for being evil, she had such an awful hoarseness in her voice, it made Jakko cringe.

In Wonder Valley, it was always warm and beautiful. There was never a season such as winter, because long, long ago, a sorcerer had put a spell on the land. He had captured winter and placed it into a magical snow globe. Sheena desperately wanted to steal it, because her power would increase with its magic, and she could finally destroy Wonder Valley. But the king had locked the snow globe in a secret room within the castle, keeping it safe from ever falling into the wrong hands. Sheena was always trying to think of ways to sneak into the castle without being caught, but it was always too risky, especially since no one ever seemed to leave the castle.

"Someone is coming!" said Jakko. Sheena and Jakko quickly went inside their home and peeked through a small hole of the tree. They watched as Princess Ezrah rode past on her horse, with Beeley now sitting proudly on Tulip's head. Sheena stared in awe, surprised to see that Ezrah was away from the castle with her guardian Beeley.

"It cannot be!" Sheena said with an evil smirk on her face. "The princess away from her castle? And her guardian Beeley too?" She looked at Jakko, smiling wickedly as she picked him up by his long ears. "A great opportunity has arisen for us Jakko. We mustn't pass it up." She let go of Jakko, dropping him as if she forgot she was even holding him.

Sheena paced back and forth, pressing her finger to her cracked lips, frowning, and thinking hard. "Hmmm… But how do I get in the castle without being suspected?"

She looked out the hole of the tree once more to observe Ezrah and Beeley. They were almost out of sight when an idea sprung within Sheena's corrupted mind. "That's it!" She laughed. "Oh, it will be so easy!"

Jakko looked up at Sheena, confused.

"I will simply turn myself into an owl, an owl that looks exactly like Beeley. That way, I can sneak into the castle without getting caught. I will just have to figure out where that snow globe is kept. And once I do, there will be nothing wondrous about Wonder Valley again!" Sheena laughed the most evil and dark laugh, which made Jakko's whole body quiver with fear, causing his back leg to thump uncontrollably.

"Come on, Jakko! We must get moving. We haven't much time," Sheena said impatiently.

And so the evil witch cast a spell on herself. She started transforming into some kind of creature as black smoke swirled around her, until finally POOF! Jakko covered his eyes by holding his long ears over them with his paws. He finally decided to peek, but Sheena was nowhere to be found. Suddenly he heard a SWOOP and something grabbed onto his ears, lifting him up so he was suspended in midair.

Sheena had turned herself into an owl that looked exactly like Beeley. But she still had the same voice. "Let's go visit the castle, shall we, Jakko? It's long overdue," Sheena said, laughing. She then flew through the forest and toward the castle, clinging to Jakko's ears as she carried him with her.

Chapter 4
Castle Break-In

Sheena arrived at the castle and dropped Jakko near the front gates, which blocked off the path leading up to the huge entrance doors.

"I need a distraction for those dumb mutts down there," Sheena yelled as she looked down at Jakko.

Jakko tensed up, frightened at the thought of being a *distraction* or maybe even dinner for the two bobcats, Tony and Tray.

"Did you hear that?" Tony, the very large bobcat, asked.

"Yeah, I heard something over there by the trees," replied Tray.

"It better not be those wild squirrels again!" Tony warned, rubbing the top of his sore head.

The two bobcats headed over to where Jakko had been dropped. Jakko heard Tony and Tray coming and hopped across the green velvety grass toward a hole in an old pine tree.

"Let's get him!" yelled Tray in excitement, catching sight of Jakko.

Seeing Tony and Tray coming at him, Jakko then zipped across the grass as fast as he could, keeping his dangly ears back so he wouldn't trip over them. Tony and Tray chased him to the pine tree and almost had him before Jakko slipped into the hole.

"Aw…maybe next time," Tray said as he laughed at Tony spitting out some hair he had bit off Jakko's puffy white tail.

"Yuck…" Tony said, coughing up Jakko's hair and pawing at his tongue. "Stupid rabbits."

Sheena had flown through Ezrah's bedroom window, unseen by the two bobcats. She made her way to the large dining area where Princess Ezrah's family sat during mealtimes. Flying silently down a long hallway, she eventually reached a huge winding staircase. She perched on the railing, staying very still as she listened to nearby voices.

"Have you seen Ezrah?" asked the king. "I would like to go over some things before she makes her final decision on who she wishes to marry."

"I haven't seen her. I am sure she's around here somewhere. She has a lot to think about in a very short amount of time," replied the queen.

"And that is why I wish to speak with her. She must choose a prince who can be trusted, for they will be gaining a huge responsibility securing the snow globe," the king said sternly.

Sheena's big bulgy eyes got bigger as she heard the king mention the snow globe. She kept completely still upon the railing. She hoped the king would give some sort of clue to where the snow globe was kept.

"Yes, but you know what happens when you try to persuade her to agree with you," the queen said. "She will only rebel more."

"Maybe I should just order her to marry the one I choose for her," said the king.

"An arranged marriage?" asked the queen, surprised.

"Why not? That's how it was done in the past."

"Yes, but forcing her to marry someone she does not choose herself will only result in chaos."

"Oh, there will be plenty of chaos, dear queen," Sheena whispered to herself. "And once I get a hold of the snow globe, there will be no need for Ezrah to marry, for I will be ruler of Wonder Valley!" She stretched out her wings in triumph.

A few maids suddenly appeared, coming from the dining hall and walking toward Sheena. Sheena just froze with her wings still stretched out, which looked very odd. But the maids only glanced at her and continued walking, thinking she was Beeley just being weird.

"Now I must find that snow globe," Sheena said as the maids went into the kitchen to prepare for dinner. Sheena then took off and flew up the winding staircase to the top, finally making her way over to the tower.

Chapter 5
Golden Brick

Ezrah, Tulip, and Beeley eventually reached the small village of Golden Brick. They strolled into the town and were amazed by all the townspeople roaming the streets, buying and selling all sorts of knickknacks and various types of food. Many of them seemed quite happy as they talked and laughed amongst themselves.

Ezrah rode Tulip along the golden-colored brick streets and stopped in front of a large sign posted on a tree reading:

Spring Dance Festival!

Eight o'clock tonight in the town park.

Food, games, music, and of course: DANCING!

"We shall attend this party," announced Ezrah, smiling as she looked down at her horse and over at Beeley, who was still resting on Tulip's head.

Moving past the sign, they came to a huge water fountain with a statue of a cowboy and cowgirl in a dancing pose at the center. Beeley flew to the top of the statue and perched on the cowboy's hat. He kicked his feet out and slid around the cowboy hat, trying to dance, hoping to get some laughs out of Ezrah, but she only stared at him awkwardly.

Ezrah quickly turned around, hearing a loud noise behind her. A young man was riding on his horse, appearing to be chasing a small pig. Ezrah's horse was startled and jumped up, causing Ezrah to lose her balance. She fell off Tulip and landed in the water fountain.

Entirely drenched, Ezrah stood up fast, stunned by what had just happened. The man stopped his horse and turned around toward Ezrah, realizing he had caused her to fall. He jumped off his horse and went to her, holding out his hand to help her out of the fountain.

"Gosh, I am sorry, ma'am," the man said as he tried not to chuckle at the sight of Ezrah dripping wet. "I shouldn't have stormed past you like that. I just get so caught up in the game."

"Game?" Ezrah asked as she took his hand and stepped out of the fountain. Ezrah wiped the water away from her eyes and made sure her hair was still intact. She was ready to yell at the man and go ballistic. But, getting a closer look at the man, she was startled to see it was Jacob. Afraid he would recognize her, she took a step back and ended up tripping over her dress. She was just about to fall in the fountain again, but Jacob reached out his hand and grabbed her.

"If ya wanna go swimmin', I know a good lake nearby," he said with a smile.

Ezrah, somewhat annoyed, only gave a slight smile and began ringing out her dress. "You play games with a pig?" Ezrah asked sarcastically.

"Yeah, I sort of play this game now and then with Fred." The man pointed up ahead to where his pig had run. He was sitting under an old oak tree that was all by itself at the top of a hill. "If Fred my pig gets to that oak tree before I can catch 'im with this rope, he wins." The man held up his looped rope to show Ezrah. "But the tricky part is, I gotta rope im' while riding this ole horse of mine."

Jacob leaned against his horse and watched Ezrah continue ringing out her wet dress.

"I've never met a cowboy. Do they all talk like you?" Ezrah asked, trying to divert attention away from her.

"I am assuming you mean my slang?" Jacob asked raising an eyebrow. "Ha, it's inconsistent compared to most cowboys. My pa was a full out cowboy and full of slang, but then there was my ma; always speakin' proper English.

Ezrah was trying to think of a question to ask about his parents, but then Jacob suddenly leaned away from his horse and moved closer to Ezrah. "Say, you look kinda familiar. Have I seen you somewhere before?" Jacob asked suspiciously.

Ezrah panicked, trying to think of what to say, but luckily the sight of Beeley distracted him from receiving an answer, at least right away.

"Hey, aren't you Princess Ezrah's owl?" Jacob asked, looking up at Beeley who was sitting on top of Tulips head. Beeley lifted his wings and covered his eyes, thinking this whole thing was a disaster unraveling.

"What in the world are you doin' way out here?" Jacob questioned.

"Oh...yeah, that's Beeley." Ezrah interrupted. "Princess Ezrah lets him follow me when I leave to run errands for her," Ezrah said, quickly trying to come up with a believable story. Beeley uncovered his eyes, but looked guilty as Ezrah continued. "I am...uh...I am Brick. I work at the castle as a maid."

She stuck out her hand, waiting for Jacob to shake it, but he wasn't totally convinced by her story and kept his arms crossed. I work there too, but I reckon I've never seen you before," Jacob stated, "and what kind of *errand* would ya be runnin' for Ezrah in Golden Brick?"

"Oh...well..." Ezrah stuttered, "I am fairly new there, and I am usually pretty busy....not many people see me, kept hidden in the castle and all. Ezrah heard about the dance festival going on here to-night and wanted me to inspect it. She said someone had told her it was better than the parties held at the castle."

"Hmmm...she told you that, huh? Does seem like Ezrah to go and send someone to spy for her," Jacob said, surly.

He then took off his hat and pressed it to his chest. "The names Jacob; and I do apologize for how we ended up meeting today," he said, finally shaking Ezrah's hand.

"Nice to meet you Jacob, and that's okay about the dress," Ezrah said, thankful it wasn't one of her real princess dresses, "my dress will dry. No harm done."

"Well...Brick, let me make it up to you and get you some dry clothes. I bet my sisters can find ya somethin' nice to wear," Jacob said, getting back on his horse. "Follow me. I live just a little ways past that hill up there."

Ezrah looked down at herself and realized she was too much of a mess to go to the festival later. Plus, it was her chance to find out more about Jacob. Ezrah accepted Jacob's request and got back on Tulip. Beeley shook his head in disagreement, but followed anyway.

Jacob and Ezrah rode up the hill to where Fred the pig was and followed him through a small field and then across a narrow stream. It didn't take long before they came to Jacob's small ranch.

A huge white house and a barn almost the same size towered over the land, both built on a hill. Fence outlined all the land Jacob's family owned, with cows and horses scattered about. All sorts of pretty trees with flowers were found throughout, dandelions covered up most of the grass that was the lawn, and every so often the wind would break off the old white tops and wisp them along.

"This place is wonderful," Ezrah said, amazed by the animals and the peacefulness of it all. It reminded her much of Wonder Valley.

"It's not so bad," Jacob replied. "Come on, let's go inside."

Jacob helped Ezrah off her horse, and she looked into his beautiful blue eyes. She suddenly felt a little weak and stumbled into his arms.

"Sorry," she said, feeling embarrassed.

"Are you sure you work at the castle? You sure don't seem very steady on your feet," Jacob teased.

"Yeah, just a little off balance lately..." Ezrah said, feeling her cheeks get red and hot, which was a weird feeling. Ezrah was never embarrassed. She was the princess! She was so confused how different her emotions were around Jacob.

Jacob chuckled. "Come on," he said and took her hand, leading her toward the house. There on the front porch was Fred the pig. "I'll get you next time," said Jacob. Fred only snorted back at him, doubting he ever would.

Chapter 6
Sheena Steals the Snow Globe

Sheena had made her way to the castle tower, finding the only room that was locked. She knew the snow globe was probably within it. She just needed to find the key.

"Where is that blasted key?" Sheena said, frustrated. She flew around, looking in every nook and cranny and in all the rooms surrounding the tower. She perched up above a chandelier that hung below a glass window. Sheena looked down, wondering where the key could be hidden, when something glistening caught her eye. She noticed one of the crystal icicles of the chandelier was reflecting colors of the rainbow, when none of the other crystals did.

Clever, Sheena thought. She grabbed the piece of chandelier with her talons and broke it off. She then plunged down toward the room and fit the crystal into the key hole. With a slight turn the door unlocked and swung open.

"Yes!" Sheena whooed. There in the middle of the room on a sculpted stone pedestal was the magical snow globe. She flew toward it, clasped it tightly, and flew as fast as she could out of the room and out of the castle.

Sheena arrived at her tree, and moments after entering it, the magic spell wore off and she returned to her human form. Jakko was there waiting for her return after he luckily escaped the castle grounds.

"Ahh…Jakko," said Sheena in her dark, low voice, "finally! My time has come to rule over Wonder Valley!"

Jakko kept thumping his legs nervously while Sheena began casting her spells on the snow globe. He was frightened of this new power Sheena had gained and how she was going to use it.

Chapter 7
Jacob & Ezrah

Jacob and Ezrah entered the house, while Beeley stayed outside on the porch. Fred the pig sat tall and proud, acting like a guardian just like Beeley. Beeley puffed out his chest even more, but Fred only mimicked him further.

Jacob and Ezrah walked into the kitchen, where Jacob's two sisters were. They were washing dishes and laughing at their own jokes.

"These are my sisters, Julia and Becca," Jacob introduced.

The two sisters were startled at the sound of his voice. They turned around to face Jacob and were so bewildered to see a girl standing next to him that they both dropped a dish. The dishes fell to the ground, breaking in a few shards, yet the sisters acted like nothing happened. They were too mesmerized by the presence of another girl in the house.

"Hi!" Julia and Becca both said at the same time. Ezrah introduced herself as Brick, shaking their hands pleasantly.

"Where are you from?" Julia asked Ezrah.

"Uh…" Ezrah didn't know what to say. She had to try and remember what she had told Jacob and stick to the same story. "I am from Wonder Valley," she finally said.

"Wonder Valley!" the two sisters yelled in excitement at the same time. "Wowee! What are you doing here in this small town?" asked Becca.

"Well, um…I am just…just going out for the day. I heard there was a dance festival here tonight and thought it would be fun to come," Ezrah said quietly.

"So you were hoping to meet someone then." Julia nudged Jacob's arm. "Jacob would love to take you to the dance tonight," she said and Becca agreed.

Becca and Julia shot a glance at Jacob, hinting that he should ask Ezrah to go with him.

"Yeah, I could take you…if you don't mind." Jacob ran his hand through his dark brown hair.

"I suppose you could," Ezrah said with a smile.

"Well, come on then!" said Julia, pulling Ezrah along and leading her upstairs. "Let's find you something to wear!"

Jacob remained downstairs and went into his room to get ready for the dance. Upstairs, the sisters picked out dresses for Ezrah to try on.

Becca grabbed the two dresses Jacob had bought for her and Julia, showing them off to Ezrah. "Don't we have the best brother?" she said without expecting a response.

"Yes, a sweet, very *single* brother," Julia answered her. The sisters looked at each other and then at Ezrah with a huge smirk across their faces.

The sisters continued to analyze each dress in the closet before finally picking out a blue country-style one, ruffled just above the knees where the dress stopped. Julia picked out some matching cowgirl boots, while Becca did Ezrah's hair in a long spiral ponytail.

After they were all done, Becca and Julia pulled Ezrah over to a mirror to look at herself. Ezrah couldn't believe how strange she appeared. She would have never guessed that underneath this ridiculous outfit was a princess. The ungrateful princess side of her came out when she scowled and said, "Do you not have a dress more fit for going out in public?"

The two sisters looked at each other, puzzled.

"This is the best dress we have," Becca muttered.

"Well, besides the dresses Jacob bought us," Julia pointed out.

"This one was our mother's favorite," added Becca.

Ezrah's scowl quickly faded. "*Was?*"

"Our parents passed away when we were seven," said Becca,

staring down at the floor in front of her. "Big storm came and sunk the ship they were on."

"Oh, I am sorry," Ezrah said sympathetically.

The twins just nodded their heads. After a few moments of silence, Ezrah began swaying back and forth in front of the mirror. "You know, looking more at the dress and moving in it, I think you both picked me out the perfect one for a dance festival," said Ezrah, hoping to lighten the mood and make up for her rude comment about the dress. "It really is stunning."

Becca and Julia looked at Ezrah with huge smiles, both jumping up and down with excitement and clapping their hands.

"Wait until Jacob sees you!" Becca squealed.

Becca and Julia brought Ezrah downstairs to Jacob. He was sitting at the kitchen table, buffing up his cowboy boots and making them shine. When Jacob looked up at Ezrah, he couldn't stop staring at her, for he had never seen anyone so beautiful.

Becca and Julia gave each other a wink.

"You guys go. We will meet you at the dance later," said Julia.

Ezrah and Jacob went outside to grab the horses and go back into town, but Jacob couldn't catch his horse. He chased him all over the field, but his horse kept running away, as if he were playing some type of silly game. Tulip walked over to Jacob and nudged him in the back. Jacob turned around to see Tulip holding part of his own horse reigns in his mouth. "So, I am hitching a ride with you eh?" Jacob said to Tulip. Tulip nudged him again, and as if he were taking an order from a horse, Jacob then climbed up on Tulips back and rode over to Ezrah.

"Hey pretty girl," Jacob said enticing, "need a lift?"

"Sure...," Ezrah hesitated. "As long as I don't get dumped into a water fountain again."

"Not with me you won't," replied Jacob, lowering his hand down to Ezrah to help her up.

She grabbed it reluctantly, and with one swift movement Jacob swung her up so she was sitting behind him. "How fast does this horse go?"

"I don't know, and I don't care to find out."

She had barely even finished her sentence when Jacob yelled for her to hang on. He swiftly tapped Tulip's sides with the heels of his boots and urged Tulip to run his fastest. Ezrah screamed at first, but then began to laugh. She had never felt so wild and free. Beeley flew behind, flapping his wings hard as he struggled to keep up. Fred the pig stayed on the porch snorting loudly. He didn't feel like running again.

Chapter 8

Dance Festival

Tulip ran full speed right through town, Ezrah wailing in slight screams and laughter. Jacob brought Tulip to an abrupt halt once they reached the fountain Ezrah had fallen into earlier that day. The fountain was the center of the town square, and it was where the dance festival was being held. All sorts of townspeople mingled about, talking and laughing amongst themselves and eating all kinds of foods.

"Dancing should be startin' soon. You're gonna love it. We all get pretty rowdy," said Jacob, helping Ezrah down off Tulip.

Ezrah gazed around, studying the dresses the women and young girls were wearing. She could tell by observation that these people had little money, not only by the clothes they wore, but for the simple decorations hung so sparingly on surrounding trees and the boring presentation of food choices; yet everyone appeared to be having a great time.

"Come on! You gotta try some of the food," Jacob said, taking

Ezrah's hand and pulling her over to the long table with all the food atop. "All of it is homemade, and you ain't never had anything as good as these here rhubarb sticks." Jacob pointed to the basket that held the sweets.

Doubtfully, Ezrah grabbed one of the rhubarb sticks and took a bite off the end. Surprisingly, her cringing, worried face quickly relaxed when the sweet, sugary flavor awakened every one of her taste buds.

"Oh my! This is absolutely delicious!" Ezrah said aloud. Jacob only chuckled and agreed with her. Ezrah couldn't stop eating them. They were the best-tasting sweet she had ever had. "These had to have come from Wonder Valley, but what shop?" she asked.

"Ha, they didn't come from Wonder Valley or any store. Like I said, everything is homemade. Somebody made 'em and brought 'em to share tonight."

Ezrah couldn't believe how many people must have participated in providing all the various food items.

"It's the same with everything else you be seein' here," Jacob added, "decorations, music, games. Everyone helps out and we have fun with what we have."

And what these people had was hardly anything, but they all

seemed happy. Ezrah started to question her own happiness and how she felt empty and alone most of the time, though she had always had everything she ever desired. She always had the best dress, best hairdo, best shoes, best everything when it came to *things*. Ezrah suddenly longed to feel the joy that surrounded her in the small town of Golden Brick.

Chapter 9
Sheena Takes Over Wonder Valley

The king and queen went searching for Ezrah in the castle when she didn't show up for dinner. They came to the secret room and saw the door was unlocked. The king and queen became frantic. The snow globe had been stolen, and their daughter was missing.

Ezrah's parents ordered their guards Tony and Tray, the bobcats, to search for Ezrah in the kingdom. The king also told the kingdom's soldiers to prepare to fight and protect the people from any harm.

The king and queen watched out the castle windows, hoping for Ezrah's return. They became quite frightened when they saw snow begin to fall from the dark, cloudy sky. Wind whirled through Wonder Valley and ripped all the flowers off their stems. Snow came down harder and harder, covering all Wonder Valley's beauty and making it impossible to see very far.

"Sheena..." the king growled in anger. He knew she must have stolen the snow globe.

"What are we going to do?" the queen cried helplessly.

Suddenly they both heard the castle doors open and close, and they ran to them, thinking it might be Ezrah. But to their surprise it was Sheena the witch. She strode in with her long, dark black dress, tinted with dark streaks of blue trailing on the floor behind her. Jakko, covered in snow, flopped his ears a few times and thumped his thumpers to shake it all off.

"Sheena..." the king said in disgust.

"It's been a while, dear king. Have you missed me?" Sheena asked, laughing. "You see, I have the power now, and my time has finally come to rule this kingdom!" She strolled around as she picked up different objects to look at.

"If you think we are just going to stand back and let you ruin Wonder Valley, you are way out of your mind," Ezrah's father proclaimed.

"Oh, I *do* think you will stand back and let me take over, because if you don't...I will create a blizzard so strong, it will wipe out everyone and everything!" Sheena replied. She twirled her dress, and a blast of ice-cold wind sent the king and queen tumbling over.

The king got up and brushed off the small speckles of ice that covered his clothes. "What do you want, Sheena?" he asked desperately.

"I want you to give up your crown in front of the kingdom, declaring to all that I am the new ruler."

"They won't want you as their ruler!" the king snapped back.

"I don't think they really have a choice, do they?" Sheena laughed, pointing out the window with her wand. There in the front yard were a number of soldiers, frozen and turned to ice.

Sheena took her wand and pointed it out the window at the soldier ice sculptures, doing her evil magic. In only a moment, the ice soldiers became mobile and marched into the castle. The king stepped in front of the queen, ready to protect her and to fight.

"These two are prisoners," Sheena said, pointing at the king and queen. "Take them to the tower so I can lock them up."

The king drew his sword, but one of the ice soldiers grabbed it before he could swing. The other two ice soldiers restrained the king and queen and led them upstairs. The king and queen tried to escape their grasp, but it was no use. The soldiers were even stronger in their ice form.

Chapter 10
The Snowstorm

The music rumbled throughout the streets, and the people of Golden Brick cheered in excitement. Everyone began dancing in circles around the fountain, moving so freely and gliding along in unison.

"Come on," Jacob said, holding out his hand. "I will show you how we get rowdy around here."

Jacob grabbed Ezrah's hand and wrapped his other arm around her waist. He quickly two-stepped out into the crowd of dancers. He led Ezrah around in circles, dipping her down and back up as they moved about. The movements were so carefree, so opposite from the style of dancing Ezrah was used to. As Jacob continued to jostle her around, Ezrah caught sight of Beeley dancing atop the cowboy statue once again. This time, however, Ezrah laughed.

The music changed and Jacob and Ezrah, along with the rest of the townspeople, swayed back and forth slowly. Jacob looked into Ezrah's eyes, and her heart fluttered. She knew she liked Jacob, but if given more time, she was pretty sure she would fall in love with him.

Just when Jacob was about to kiss Ezrah, a huge, icy cold gust of wind whipped through, causing Jacob to lose his cowboy hat. Everyone rubbed the goose bumps that arose on their arms and looked around in confusion. Suddenly more cold wind came, and dark clouds hovered above the town of Golden Brick.

"That's weird. We haven't had a storm here for ages," said Jacob, looking up at the sky.

Suddenly, white cold and wet speckles shot down from the sky in a rage. People were in awe as they watched a blanket of white beginning to cover the ground.

"SNOW!" someone yelled in a shrill voice.

Wind picked up and the snow began to mix with ice and fell harder and harder. Everyone scattered and took cover in various stores.

"Let's get out of this mess!" said Jacob, taking Ezrah's hand and making her run with him to a nearby shop. They stood underneath an overhang and watched the blizzard unravel before them.

"Something is terribly wrong!" Ezrah said, rubbing her arms, which were beginning to feel quite cold.

"There's definitely somethin' wrong, all right. Snow is somethin' ya only read about in history books. Jacob noticed that when he exhaled, he could see his breath.

Beeley flew underneath the overhang where Ezrah and Jacob were, with Tulip following right behind.

"Princess! We have to get back to the kingdom!" Beeley said, frantically flapping his wings.

"Princess? Why did he call you Princess?" Jacob asked.

Beeley sat on Tulip's head and covered his eyes with his wings. He knew he had blown Ezrah's cover.

Ezrah looked up at Jacob apologetically. She knew it was time to tell him the truth. She slowly removed her wig, revealing her long, curly blonde hair.

Jacob's eyes grew wide. "Are you kidding me? It was you all along?!" He threw his arms up in frustration.

Tulip shook the snow off his back, and with it came some of the black ash Ezrah had used to disguise him. Tulip hung his head down when Jacob glared at him with disappointment.

"Wow. Even the horse fooled me," Jacob said.

"I am sorry I didn't tell you who I really was, but I just needed to take a break from being a princess."

"You needed a *break?* What, "princess life" too hard for you?" Jacob asked sarcastically.

Ezrah felt insulted. "You have no clue what it's like being a princess! And you have no clue what people expect from me!"

"Expectations of kindness must be pretty tough for you," Jacob fired back.

The snow continued to fall heavily. There was no way of getting back to the kingdom in the middle of a blizzard. Ezrah knew arguing with Jacob wasn't going to solve anything at the moment, so she went inside the small shop where several of the townspeople lingered. Jacob soon followed behind, while Tulip and Beeley remained under the overhang.

A short, chipper young woman handed out blankets. She held one up to Jacob and Ezrah, and they both grabbed it at the same time. Ezrah quickly released her grip. "You take it," she said to Jacob.

"The princess is showing kindness? Someone write this down." Jacob said harshly.

Ezrah whipped the blanket back out of Jacob's hands. "Fine!" she yelled. "Think of me how you want!" She stared intensely at Jacob, and his face softened when he saw her eyes begin to water.

Ezrah quickly turned around, embarrassed by yet another emotion she never expressed. Jacob seemed to have the power of channeling all sorts of emotions in Ezrah she often hid, covering them up with the riches of royalty.

Jacob was about to reach his hand out to her, but she quickly walked away to the opposite side of the shop to find a place to rest. The townspeople scattered about as well, claiming an area on the floor to lie upon. Jacob stayed put, regretting some of the things he said to Ezrah, and he sat in a chair and closed his eyes to sleep. Ezrah tried sleeping as well, but worrying about what was going on back home in her kingdom kept her up most of the night.

Morning came, and Beeley flew into the shop to wake up Ezrah, frightening her as usual. Ezrah snuck out of the shop without waking the rest of the sleeping townsfolk, for the sun hadn't even come up yet. The snowstorm was over and luckily the cold that came with it had ended. It felt like it usually felt outside—warm—but everything had lost its color, hidden underneath piles of snow.

Ezrah got on her horse, knowing she had to get back to the kingdom fast.

"What are ya finin to do?" asked Jacob, closing the shop door behind him and rubbing his tired eyes.

"I am going back to Wonder Valley. I have a horrible feeling this snowstorm has something to do with a witch," replied Ezrah.

"Witch?" Jacob said, raising his eyebrows.

"Sheena...a witch my father has warned me about all my life. I should have never left the castle." Ezrah looked down, feeling guilty. "I am not the horrible princess you think I am; at least not anymore," she added. "Coming to Golden Brick made me realize I needed to change."

Then, giving Tulip a slight kick with her heels, she yelled out a good-bye to Jacob. Ezrah was out of Jacob's sight within seconds, for Tulip knew she had to run her fastest. Beeley turned around and looked at Jacob, giving him another wink before catching up with Ezrah and Tulip. Jacob tapped his foot while crossing his arms, taking a few moments to decide what he should do next.

Chapter 11
Wonder Valley Restored

"Dang-nabbit," Jacob said aloud, knowing he must go after Ezrah and admitting to himself he truly liked her. He then left the overhang of the shop. "Where'd my hat fly off to?" he grumbled.

Jacob found it hanging on the hands of the cowboy and cowgirl statue. He brushed off the snow and put it on. "Can't go on fightin' some witch without proper attire."

Just then, he heard stomping of hooves behind him. He turned around to find his horse running toward him, with his sisters riding on its back. Becca and Julia jumped off after the horse skidded to a stop on the slippery snow.

"Look who decided to show up to the after party!" Jacob joked. "What you two doin' out in this natural disaster?"

"We were about to leave, but then the snowstorm hit!" Becca said, angrily looking around at all the snow. "We didn't even get to show off our pretty dresses!"

"Where is Brick?" asked Julia.

"Ha. Don't you mean Ezrah?" said Jacob. "She was disguising herself."

The sisters turned to each other and gasped.

"Oh my gosh!" Becca and Julia screamed simultaneously. They looked at each other and squealed in excitement that they had met the princess and she was at *their* house.

"Okay, before y'all get crazy about this whole deal, I gotta go after her. She may be in some real trouble," said Jacob, getting on his horse. "Wow, you remembered to bring my rope too?" he said in amazement as he noticed it hanging off the saddle horn.

"You always have it with you. Figured you forgot it and might need it," said Becca.

Jacob thanked his sisters and then ordered them to go into one of the shops and wait with some of the townsfolk until his return. Becca and Julia pouted and pleaded to go with him, but Jacob ignored them and took off on his horse into the white forest.

Ezrah, Tulip, and Beeley entered the kingdom, which was now covered with snow. Icicles hung from the roofs of shops along the streets. The kingdom appeared deserted. Ezrah figured everyone was inside their homes. They rode further into the kingdom, and there at the gated entrance were Tony and Tray. But they had become like statues, having been turned to ice.

"Oh no!" Ezrah gasped in fear.

Beeley flapped his wings up in disbelief, and Tulip trotted quickly past. As they got closer to the castle, they saw many more ice sculptures; they were the castle soldiers.

"They were getting prepared to fight," said Ezrah.

"This isn't good, Princess. Somebody, probably a certain witch, has taken over Wonder Valley," Beeley ventured.

"My parents!" the princess said worriedly. "We must find them!"

Beeley led the way toward the castle with Ezrah and Tulip close behind. She got off her horse and ran to the castle doors. Before she could open them though, two ice soldiers came running at her as if they were attacking. Tulip ran toward one, turned around quickly, and kicked, but the ice soldier didn't even flinch. Beeley pecked at the other, but it was no use. The soldiers were too strong and they captured Ezrah.

"They are under some type of spell!" Ezrah yelled out at Beeley and Tulip. "Get out of here and get help!"

Just then, the castle doors opened and Sheena came out in her long, dark black dress. Her hair appeared stiff and unmoving, almost like the icicles that hung from the length of her dress. Tulip and Beeley went off to hide before Sheena spotted them. Ezrah stood still while the soldiers at each side of her held her arms back.

"Well, well, well…if it isn't the lovely Princess Ezrah. So nice of you to return," Sheena said with a huge smirk planted across her face.

"What do you want? Where are my parents?!" Ezrah demanded.

"What I want is to rule over Wonder Valley, which I am actually doing at the moment if you haven't noticed," said Sheena, waving her wand around and flaunting herself as she walked back and forth, "and don't worry about your parents, little princess. They are safe…locked up." Sheena gave a crackling laugh.

Ezrah became so upset that she was able to break free from the two soldiers. She moved quickly toward Sheena, ready to try to take her down. But Sheena quickly raised her wand and pointed it at Ezrah, zapping her with magic and turning her into another ice sculpture.

"Oh, what a beautiful lawn ornament. Don't you agree Jakko?" Sheena proudly announced. She laughed hysterically, caressing Ezrah's frozen face in mockery. Jakko raised his ears and they shook from the loudness of her laugh. His thumpers couldn't stop thumping, causing him to kick up snow and hop oddly as he followed Sheena and her wicked laugh back into the castle.

It wasn't long before Jacob reached Wonder Valley. His horse slowed to a walk, having trouble trudging through the deeper snow covering the kingdom. Everything that made Wonder Valley beautiful was now covered in white and glazed over with ice. Jacob and his horse finally reached the castle grounds and noticed everything appeared vacant, except for the frozen ice sculpture soldiers and bobcats, Tony and Tray. Riding up to the castle doors, Jacob spotted a beautiful ice sculpture resembling a young woman. He got off his horse and went over to it, studying the resemblance of Ezrah.

"Oh no!" Jacob gasped, realizing it really was Ezrah, frozen to ice.

Beeley flew from the tree he was hiding in and perched on frozen Ezrah's outstretched arm. "Sheena the witch has taken over Wonder Valley," Beeley said. "Anyone whoooo gets in her way she turns to ice! Like Princess Ezrah." Beeley's eyes drooped as sadness overwhelmed him.

Jacob looked up at Beeley and back down to Ezrah. He, too, felt sad and defeated. "How do we stop her?"

"I think she gets her power from the magic snow globe, a globe that traps winter. It belongs to the king, but somehow Sheena found a way to steal it. After sneaking into the castle and spying on her, I've noticed she always has it with her."

"Well then, I guess we'll just have to steal it back then, now won't we," said Jacob, pressing his hat down firmly on his head.

Jacob caressed Ezrah's face, feeling horrible he couldn't have reached her sooner to protect her. He didn't know why, but he had the sudden urge to kiss her. Jacob leaned down and gave Ezrah a soft and quick kiss.

Almost instantly, ice began melting from her face and hair, moving down her back, and then out her arms and down her legs. The care that was expressed in the warmth of Jacob's kiss had broken the evil spell and melted the ice away.

Beeley flapped his wings and flew up in the air. Ezrah, stunned to see Jacob standing right in front of her, wrapped her arms tightly around him. Jacob hugged her back, almost gasping for air.

"Jacob!" Ezrah yelled in excitement. "You came after me."

"Yeah, well...I figured ya needed a cowboy's help," he said.

"My parents...we have to save them! This is my fault and I have to make it right," Ezrah said.

"It's not your fault! It was only a matter a time before someone like Sheena woulda stolen that globe thing. Now let's get rowdy, eh?" Jacob said lightheartedly.

Beeley flew above Jacob and Ezrah as they headed toward the castle doors. An ice soldier quickly ran toward them, raising his sword and about to strike Ezrah, but Jacob swung his rope and snatched it from him. Beeley dropped a net on the ice soldier, wrapping the end of it on Tulip's saddle horn. Tulip dragged the soldier through the gates and out into the kingdom. Jacob held the sword high in the air, breaking through the castle doors with Ezrah at his side.

They entered and shifted their eyes in every direction, waiting to be detected, but there was no one. "Come on," Jacob said in a whisper. "Let's check upstairs."

Jacob led the way with Ezrah following closely behind, quietly making their way up the stairs. They came to the top and swiftly moved down the hallway, peeking in each room for the king and queen.

"I bet they are in the tower room," Ezrah said knowingly.

Ezrah and Jacob hurried down the hallway toward the tower, going into the room that once kept the snow globe hidden. There within the room was a prison cell made of ice bars and caged within it were the king and queen.

"Mom! Dad!" Ezrah yelled, running toward them.

"Ezrah..." the king and queen said together in relief.

"How do we get ya outta here? There some type a key?" Jacob asked anxiously.

"There is no key," the king replied, "only magic. You must get the snow globe back from Sheena and somehow destroy it."

"The only thing that will be destroyed is Wonder Valley!" Sheena said aloud, joining the rest of them in the room. Jakko hopped behind nervously, looking desperately for a place to hide.

"Let my parents go!" Ezrah threatened.

"I thought I froze you!" Sheena said in a quiver of anger and disbelief.

"Do as she said! And give back the shiny globe thing," ordered Jacob.

"Oh, you weak little commoner; trying to be the hero and impress the young princess. Such a tragedy this will be." Sheena snickered as she shook her head. "Don't worry, you will be with the princess...you will both be lovely ice sculptures!" Sheena pulled out her wand, aiming it at Jacob. Jacob acted quickly and, with his sword, blocked the zap of magic that came his way. The magic hit his sword and in a few seconds it turned to ice.

Jacob tossed the sword to Ezrah and started swinging his rope. He threw it out just in time before Sheena could zap him with her wand. The rope wrapped around the end of her wand, and Jacob snapped it back, causing the wand to slip right out from her grasp. Catching the wand, Jacob pointed it back at her. "Give us the snow globe, Sheena!"

"You fool," Sheena said, "you will have to do better than that!" She spun in a circle and her dress blasted a gust of cold wind at Jacob and Ezrah. The wind was so strong, it caused them to fall to the floor and drop the sword and wand.

"I think it's time for a blizzard," said Sheena with an evil smile growing wider across her face. She pulled out the snow globe from a pocket hidden within her dress and raised it above her head. She began spinning in circles, creating gusts of wind mixed with ice that protruded from her dress. Snow began to swarm from the globe, blasting out the roof of the castle in a tornado shape. The whirlwind of a blizzard was getting stronger, but before it could spread from the castle grounds and out to the kingdom, Beeley flew into the room and snatched the snow globe out of Sheena's hand.

"Give that back!" screamed Sheena.

Beeley flew toward Ezrah, dropping it in her open hands. Jacob and Ezrah knew they had to act fast and destroy the snow globe before Sheena could take it back from them. Jacob ran to the sword and held it firmly in his hands. Ezrah threw the snow globe toward him, and with a strong and hard swing he batted the globe, shattering it into millions of tiny pieces.

Instantly, the winter storm that Sheena had been mastering evaporated into nothing. The prison cell that held the king and queen melted and splashed into a puddle of water. Outside, all the snow had begun to retreat from the drifts and banks, finally disappearing as it melted into the ground.

"Noooo! This is my time to rule!" Sheena screamed in rage, watching her winter catastrophe vanish before her eyes. Jakko quickly scampered out of the room, hoping to be long gone before Sheena noticed. He didn't much care for Sheena and thought she was scary and crazy. Jakko knew this was the best shot he had to escape.

The king and queen rushed to Ezrah, wrapping their arms around her and holding her tight. Sheena swarmed toward her wand, tripping over her dress and falling to the floor. She stretched her arm out, reaching for the wand that was only inches from her grasp. But before her fingers could wrap around it, a cowboy boot firmly stepped on the top of the wand. Sheena looked up to see it was Jacob, pointing a sword at her that was covered in ice only moments ago. Jacob gloated and in one quick motion, he lifted his boot and then slammed it back down on the wand, cracking it in half.

A few soldiers came running up the castle stairs and into the tower room. They were back to normal now that the spell over them had been broken. Jacob handed his sword to one of the soldiers as the other two picked up Sheena and held her arms back; restraining her while she aggressively tried to pull free. The soldier holding the sword went to the king, asking him what he wanted them to do with Sheena.

"I think Sheena needs a vacation," said the king in a pleasant, but sarcastic tone. "Send her to an island that is full of wild flowers and is sunny all the time."

The soldier nodded his head and directed the other two soldiers to follow him out of the room.

Sheena's eyes grew wide with fear. "I HATE flowers!" she yelled in frustration. "I LOATHE the sun and all things beautiful!" she spat.

The two soldiers dragged her out of the castle and sent her away as the king ordered.

"I am so sorry..." cried Ezrah. "I never meant for this to happen." The king and queen hugged her tightly, thankful she had returned and that the kingdom was restored. Ezrah promised she would never act so selfishly again and reassured them she'd make things right and choose a prince to marry—a prince worthy of ruling over Wonder Valley.

Jacob overheard her and his heart sank. With more time, he knew he'd probably fall in love with Princess Ezrah. He felt he already had, but he knew it was a strict rule of the kingdom that a princess only marry a prince. Feeling hurt and not wanting any more confrontation, Jacob snuck out of the room without saying good-bye. Ezrah turned away from her parents, forgetting to include Jacob.

"Where did he go?" Ezrah asked with sadness in her voice. Beeley, who was perched on a windowsill, pointed with his wing outside. Ezrah ran to the window, looking out and seeing that Jacob was riding on his horse, heading away from the castle grounds. Ezrah frantically opened the window and called out his name over and over, yet he didn't stop. He was too far away to hear her.

"That young man; doesn't he work here?" the queen asked Ezrah.

Ezrah turned around with tears forming in her eyes. "Yes...but suddenly I wish he was a prince." She ran into her mother's arms and began to cry. The king looked at his daughter with concern and then at the queen. The queen and king gazed at each other at a distance. They had rarely seen their daughter cry and express an emotion that declared her feelings for another person. They both came to the con-clusion their daughter's heart had been touched by this young man— the young man who helped save Wonder Valley.

Chapter 12

The Grand Dinner

P rincess Ezrah sat at the head of a long dinner table, along with the twelve princes' she had danced with just a few nights ago at the Grand Ball. The king and queen sat at their own private table nearby. The table was cluttered with all sorts of food, fruit, and sweets, and it reminded Ezrah of the dance festival in Golden Brick. She scanned the table, thinking of the tasty rhubarb sticks Jacob had made her try. But there was nothing of the sort.

All the princes were talking amongst themselves, each bragging to the other about their wealth and the kingdom they are from. And, while they all seemed to be indulging in the meal set before them, Ezrah never took a single bite of hers. She was too busy scanning over each prince, trying to picture her-self being married to him or if he was even trustworthy to help rule a kingdom. Ezrah even tried to imagine each prince in a cowboy hat, but all she saw was Jacob.

Ding ding ding. The sound of a fork hitting the tip of Ezrah's glass in front of her broke her trance of daydreaming and quieted everyone in the room. The king set the fork down and stood proudly behind Ezrah with the queen.

Ezrah knew her father would give a short speech, which meant she only had a few minutes to quickly make her decision. She glanced back and forth at a few princes near her, all sending her winks and wide smiles of sparkling white teeth.

"Thank you all for coming tonight in honor of accepting my daughter's hand in marriage," the king began. "However, the queen and I have decided that forcing a marriage upon Ezrah will not enrich this kingdom, because a marriage should come out of love, and love cannot be forced."

Ezrah's mouth dropped open, along with those of the twelve princes gathered around the table.

The king continued, ignoring their responses. "We also believe Ezrah has proven she has the responsibility and courage to solely rule this kingdom in her selfless act of fighting to save it from Sheena's ruin. Therefore, instead of choosing one of you to marry, she will pick one of you as an apprentice. You will still aid her in decisions and responsibilities of the kingdom, but she will not be bonded to you under an oath. However, I do encourage Ezrah to pick an apprentice she could see herself marrying someday, but whomever she chooses to be betrothed to is her decision."

All the princes started protesting and complaining amongst themselves. The king yelled out, "HUSH!" which echoed and silenced everyone.

"Now without further ado, I leave this time for Ezrah to make her decision," said the king.

Ezrah stood up and looked at her mother and father in disbelief, making sure she wasn't just hearing things and had dreamed up what her father had just said. Her mother nodded and smiled at Ezrah. Ezrah gave her father a hug, and she was overcome by gratefulness.

Then, so no one else could hear him, the king softly said into Ezrah's ear, "A prince isn't a real prince unless he's willing to fight alongside a princess."

Ezrah was a bit confused about what her father meant. Was she supposed to pick someone like Jacob, since he fought beside her to defeat Sheena? Ezrah took a few steps away from her father and faced the table full of eager princes. She felt her stomach clench. She still had no idea which prince would best suit her. And though she didn't have to pick one to marry, she felt choosing an apprentice was equally important in the matter of ruling a kingdom.

Ezrah shot a glance over at Beeley, hoping for him to give her a clue on who she should pick. Beeley scanned the dinner table and then his eyes suddenly bulged out in surprise. Ezrah followed Beeley's line of sight onto another prince who suddenly entered the room, pulling up a chair and taking a seat at the opposite end of the dinner table. He was dressed in sleek black pants and a vest. But there was one thing about him that stood out from the rest of the princes, and that was his black cowboy boots. It didn't take very long before Ezrah realized it was Jacob, dressed as a prince. Ezrah looked up at her father, confused about what was going on.

"So, daughter, who is it you choose?" asked the king. He looked down at the other end of the table, giving a slight nod at Jacob as if hinting he had his approval. Ezrah looked down at the end of the table with a huge smile and said, "Jacob...I choose Prince Jacob."

Every prince switched their attention from Ezrah to the opposite end of the table where Jacob sat. Jacob froze, feeling all eyes on him and the glares of envy. Princes started mumbling amongst themselves, questioning who he was, for none of them had ever heard of a Prince Jacob.

Ezrah smiled at her mother and father, mouthing a "thank you."

The queen then got up and thanked all the princes for coming and ordered everyone into the ballroom. The queen grabbed Ezrah's hand, pulled her close, and said, "I am not happy about you running away from the kingdom, but I am happy you came running back, and with a changed heart." Ezrah gave her a hug, embracing the warmth and love her mother always gave.

Every prince got up from the table and huffed about not being chosen as they exited the room. Ezrah followed the king and queen out into the ballroom, where Jacob was found waiting in the middle of the dance floor. The princes crowded around in a circle to honor her decision and watch Ezrah and Jacob's first dance. Ezrah walked to Jacob and he pulled her close to him. He gave her a firm hug and Ezrah was instantly filled with happiness. They began to sway back and forth to the soft music that began to play. Jacob twirled her slowly, leading her in graceful and smooth movements.

"Have you been practicing?" Ezrah asked Jacob, impressed.

Jacob didn't answer, instead he just smiled. "By the way...," continued Ezrah, "why did you show up tonight? You must have known I would pick you, and..."

"Of course I knew you would pick me," Jacob interrupted. "Those princes hadn't a chance against a cowboy." Ezrah didn't know what to say. She could only smile back at him, because though he was being sarcastic, he was right. When the dance was over, a quick more up-beat sound of music started playing, and all kinds of people suddenly swarmed into the ballroom.

People from Wonder Valley and Golden Brick had been invited to the dance to celebrate. The people from Golden Brick began dancing the two-step, flicking up their heels and do-si-do-ing. Even Jacob's sisters Julia and Becca had come, finally able to show off the dresses Jacob had bought them. They swished side to side and clapped along to the beat of the music. Ezrah watched as the two sisters pulled a couple of princes out toward the middle of the dance floor. The princes stumbled over their own feet, trying to keep up with them. The whole scene looked incredibly awkward.

People of Wonder Valley had never seen a dance like this and were immediately enthused. Soon everyone began hopping around and moving side to side in a carefree manner. The ballroom was crammed with commoners and royalty, all having fun and laughing together.

The king and queen watched everyone from the upstairs balcony of the ballroom. They found the different style of dancing quite amusing, but what was even more amusing were the people trying to learn it. They couldn't help but laugh to themselves.

Ezrah and Jacob stopped dancing for a moment, getting lost in each other's eyes. Everyone continued to dance around them. Jacob was about to lean down and kiss Ezrah, but she quickly stood up on her tiptoes and kissed him first.

"It's only fair I take back my kiss you stole when I was frozen," Ezrah said.

She surprised Jacob, and a huge smile sprang up on his face.

"My name is Princess Ezrah," Ezrah said in a strange voice, mimicking the princes she had danced with only a few nights ago. "I do believe I am the best kisser."

Jacob spun her in a circle, dipped her down quickly and back up. "Maybe...but your dancing needs work."

Ezrah knew he was joking but frowned at him anyway. Just then, Fred the pig cut between them and moved to the middle of the dance floor. He wore a black cowboy hat and used it to express his dance moves, flinging it up in the air and sharply bringing it out to each side of him as he quickly shook his body in each direction.

Ezrah stopped, astounded. "Fred the pig can dance?!" she exclaimed in bewilderment.

"Had no idea," replied Jacob. He, too, just stopped and stared.

Beeley suddenly dropped down from above, grabbing Fred's hat and flying away with it. Fred snorted and squealed excitedly, for getting his hat back would be a challenging game to him. Fred chased Beeley throughout the ballroom, but Beeley was way too high for him to jump up and grab his hat back. Beeley eventually dropped it, but continued to fly above, enjoying his view of everyone from Wonder Valley and Golden Brick celebrating together all through the night.